D1252715

Anno's
FACES

Philomel Books   **New York**

Orange   Japanese Pear

Pear   Apple

Onion   Lemon

Radish   Turnip

Gourds

Tomato   Potato

Squash

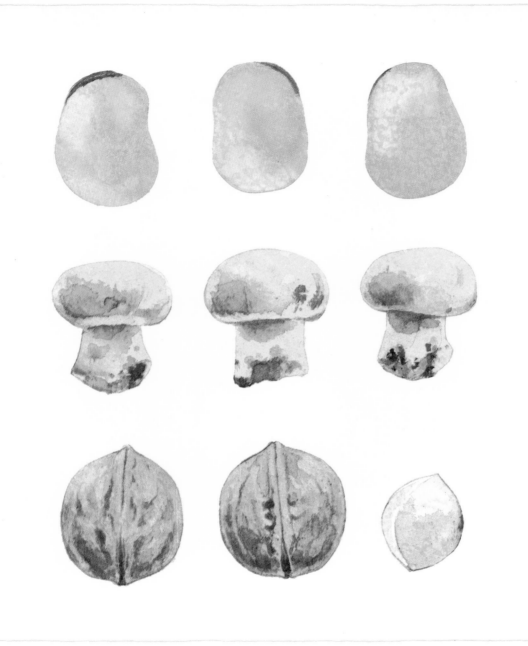

Lima Beans   Mushrooms   Walnuts   Gingko Nut

Cucumber   Carrot

Persimmon   Chestnut

Rutabaga

Cherries   Grapes

Banana   Eggplant

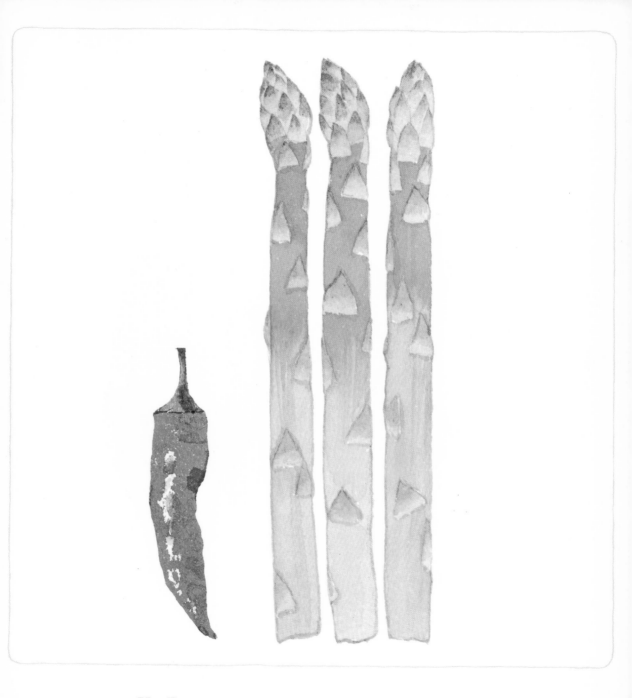

Hot Pepper   **Asparagus**

Mangosteen   Kiwi

Papaya   Avocado

Watermelon

Sweet Potato   Almonds   Peanut

Pinto Beans   Kidney Bean

Green Bell Pepper   Red Bell Pepper   Okra

Pomegranate   Fig

Peach   Plum

Cantaloupe

Mitsumasa Anno
is known the world over for his highly
original and thought-provoking picture books.
In 1984 he was awarded the Hans Christian Andersen Medal,
the highest honor attainable in the field of children's book illustration.
Born in 1926 in western Japan, Mr. Anno is a graduate of the Yamaguchi
Teacher Training College and worked for some time as a teacher before
becoming an artist. He has recently become a grandfather.
This is his second book for very young children.

English translation copyright © 1989 by Philomel Books, a division of
The Putnam & Grosset Group, 200 Madison Avenue, New York, NY 10016.
Published simultaneously in Canada. All rights reserved.
Original Japanese edition published in 1988 by Dowaya, Tokyo,
as *Nikoniko Kabocha* by Mitsumasa Anno.
Copyright © 1988 by Kūsō-Kōbō, American translation rights arranged
with Dowaya, through Japan Foreign Rights Centre. Printed in Singapore.

Library of Congress Cataloging-in-Publication Data
Anno, Mitsumasa, 1926–   Anno's faces.
Summary: Depicts familiar fruits and vegetables, including the strawberry, orange,
watermelon, and green pea. Moving see-through plastic cards over the illustrations
causes each fruit and vegetable to smile and frown.
1. Fruit — Pictorial works — Juvenile literature. 2. Vegetables — Pictorial works —
Juvenile literature. 3. Facial expression — Pictorial works — Juvenile literature.
4. Toy and movable books — Specimens. [1. Fruit. 2. Vegetables. 3. Facial expression. 4. Toy and movable books] I. Title. SB 357.2.A56 1989 88-25030.
ISBN 0-399-21711-8   First impression